The Window in the Wall

Ginny Merritt

journeyforth®

Greenville, South Carolina

Library of Congress Cataloging-in Publication Data
Merritt, Ginny, 1947-
    The window in the wall / Ginny Merritt.
        pages cm
    Summary: Relates the biblical story of Rahab, the spies,
and the fall of Jericho as recorded in the book of Joshua from
the perspective of young Talia, whose father Yakesh is one of
Rahab's brothers.
    ISBN 978-1-60682-781-9 (perfect bound pbk. : alk. paper)
— ISBN (invalid) 978-1-60682-783-3 (e-book) 1. Rahab
(Biblical figure)—Juvenile fiction. 2. Jews—History—To 1200
B.C.—Juvenile fiction. 3. Jericho—History—Siege, ca. 1400
B.C.—Juvenile fiction. [1. Rahab (Biblical figure)—Fiction. 2.
Jews—History—To 1200 B.C.—Fiction. 3. Jericho—History—
Siege, ca. 1400 B.C. 4. Family life—West Bank—Jericho—
Fiction.] I. Title.
    PZ7.M545443Win 2013
    [Fic]—dc23
                                                                        2013020671

All Scripture is quoted from the King James Version.

Cover Photos: Craig Oesterling (portrait); iStockphoto.com
© rusm (flax background), © Coica (flax plant close-up), ©
Agenturfotograf (linseed and flower), © mayang (old stone
wall)

Design by Craig Oesterling
Page layout by Michael Boone

© 2013 by BJU Press
Greenville, South Carolina 29614
JourneyForth Books is a division of BJU Press

Printed in the United States of America

ISBN 978-1-60682-781-9
eISBN 978-1-60682-783-3

15   14   13   12   11   10   9   8   7   6   5   4   3   2   1

Dedicated to my husband, Ray—
provider, protector, dearest friend on earth,
and resident theologian.

"That all the people of the earth might know
the hand of the Lord, that it is mighty:
that ye might fear the Lord your God forever."
Joshua 4:24

Contents

chapter one

The Harvest Festival

Orange flags snapped in the autumn breeze high above the mighty city walls. Talia heard the flags before she saw them in the dim light of early morning. She tilted her head back to look way up at them. It was time for the Harvest Festival.

Talia was proud of the stone walls that surrounded her city home like the strong arms of her father. Nothing could knock them down. No army could get inside the city when the big gates were closed. Talia felt safe from outside enemies.

Yet inside the walls, danger and darkness lurked. Papa did his best to protect Talia and her little brother Baka, but he couldn't keep her from having bad dreams or scary thoughts. Mama tried to protect her children too. She would sing to them at night to cover the harsh sounds of shouting and cursing in an alley near her home.

But this morning that darkness was pushed away by happy anticipation. The gates of the city would be flung open wide, and guests would stream into the marketplace. They would come to buy and trade goods, to barter and chatter with merchants and family.

"Talia!"

Mama was calling. Talia stopped gazing at the flags and hurried to catch up with her mother. They had much to do this morning to get their garment booth ready. Talia's arms were loaded with a bundle of linen tunics her mother had made to sell at the fair. Her father grew the flax outside the walls of the city. Talia was proud of the bundle she carried.

"Oops!" Talia tripped and fell over a gosling she hadn't seen. The bird squawked loudly, scolding Talia for her clumsiness. Her bundle went rolling ahead of her and just missed a mud puddle. Talia picked herself up and brushed off her own brown linen tunic.

Her elbow hurt. She had banged and scraped it on the stone pavement. She brushed some little pebbles away and felt the sting when the cool air hit the raw skin.

"Talia!" Mama called again as she rounded a corner and went out of sight. Talia retrieved her load of linen and scurried to catch up with Mama.

Once Talia had made a wrong turn when she was returning from fetching water at the well for her mother. She had gotten confused, and a gang of boys teased and taunted and then chased her. They had grabbed at her waistband and tore it off her. She had been terrified. She'd run as fast as the wind in her father's field, arriving home breathless and shaken. She didn't want to get separated from Mama now, so she moved as quickly as she could.

As Talia left the dark alley from her home near the stone tower where her aunt had an inn, she was struck by all the sounds and smells of the busy morning in the avenue of booths, shaded by stately palm trees. Kaleb the baker was steaming bread rounds over a blazing fire.

Talia realized how hungry she was. She paused to look at the stout baker at work. He was funny and friendly. When he turned and saw her with her load of tunics, he laughed and said loudly, "So, my little garment girl, how is it going this morning?"

"I am late. I tripped and scraped my elbow."

Kaleb bent forward on his short legs and examined the damage. "Ah. A wound like that on the elbow calls for some bread like this in the tummy. Here you go, my garment girl. Hurry on," and he handed her a brown roll wrapped in a green leaf, wiping his floured hands on his striped apron.

Talia munched on her warm prize as she darted around people unloading dates and olives and pigeons in cages from carts pulled by goats. Finally she came to the place where her parents always set up their booth. Her papa had already arranged the tables and racks for the tunics, shawls, and sashes across from the spot where his brother Omar would sell his honey and fruit. He had gone on to visit with his merchant friends, carrying Talia's pudgy brother Baka on his shoulders.

Her mother was carefully unfolding her load and setting out their wares. "Talia, come along, please. Take care of the waistbands and shawls. Knot them on the rope so the wind won't set them free for the taking."

"Yes, Mama. Kaleb gave me a roll. Do you want some? Look, Mama! I fell and scraped my elbow."

"Talia, you are always falling. And eating! Yes, save a bite for me. Are you all right? Don't get blood on the scarves. Here, let me bind it for you." Her busy

3

mother grabbed a long scrap of linen. She wrapped it deftly around her daughter's arm and then returned to her work.

Talia occupied herself for a while with hanging the linen scarves on the rope. Most of them were the plain tan of the natural flax fibers. The women used the plain scarves every day to tie around their waists or to hold back their hair. A few scarves had been embroidered in geometric designs by Mama on dreary winter evenings months ago. Those looked pretty among the plain ones, waving now in the breeze.

Talia had tried her hand at embroidery too. She had carefully stitched a waistband with delicate blue flax blossoms. It was a gift for her mother. Mama said it was the most beautiful waistband she ever possessed.

"Hey! Watch out!"

"Out of my way!"

The rough voices and clatter of horses' hooves on the stone pavement were followed by the sound of the braying of a donkey and the splintering of wood. Talia jerked her head around and saw that Uncle Omar had arrived with his goods and encountered some of the king's soldiers on horses that had just gone by. They had heedlessly frightened his donkey and upset the olive cart. Talia's cousin Havilah was scurrying after olives and dates rolling out of their uncle's baskets from the overturned donkey cart.

"Havilah! I'm coming! I'll help you," Talia shouted as she ran across the cobblestones.

Havilah had only a mother for a family. She used to have a twin brother, Heth, but he had died two years ago after falling off a ladder. For months since then, Havilah had spent many hours with Uncle Omar, who had no wife or children of his own. Uncle Omar was a great comfort and companion to her. He was a big man who loved to eat and laugh and hug his nieces. He always had time to talk with them. He made them each feel like they were the most important part of his day—but lonely, lovely Havilah seemed to be the apple of Uncle Omar's eye.

Uncle Omar was standing in the street, shouting and shaking his big fist at the soldiers. "Watch where you're going next time!"

Papa saw what was happening as he returned to the linen booth from visiting his friends.

"Hanah! Please take Baka," he said to his wife as he set the toddler down in her care. He joined Talia to help Omar and Havilah. The girls picked up dates and olives to save them from rolling cartwheels and careless footsteps. They held as many as they could in the folds of their tunics, and then dashed back to empty the load into baskets and boxes that had tipped out of the cart.

Some boys darted in too, to grab what they could of the spilled merchandise. Talia yelled at them. "Go away, you bad boys! Those belong to my Uncle Omar. He is bigger than you."

She stomped her foot on the pavement and spilled some of her gatherings out of her tunic. Now she would have to pick them up again. Havilah hushed her angry cousin.

"Talia. Don't worry about the ruffians. You can't stop them. Let's just try to get the rest quickly."

Meanwhile Papa and Uncle Omar examined the damage.

"What do you think, Omar? Eh? Those soldiers—they are so unconcerned with us common folks."

"Yes, yes, look at this, my brother. Several spokes on this wheel are broken and will need to be repaired before we can use it again this evening."

"Maybe you will sell all your olives and not need the cart, Omar."

"Ha, you are always the hopeful one, Yoktan. That will be the day I sell all my olives."

Talia watched her tall thin father and her plump uncle conferring. How she loved them both. The men unhitched and calmed the frightened donkey, secured him to a post, removed the broken wheel, and stabilized the cart with a wooden box. Then they left the girls to set up the honey and fruit for sale in the cart while they went off in search of a wheelwright.

Talia returned to her family's booth of garments just as the first of the customers began to stream through the gates of Jericho. It looked like a field of wildflowers with the bright garments of tribal neighbors flowing together into one tapestry.

The Harvest Festival had begun!

chapter two

A Voice in the Flax Field

"Wake up, Talia! Papa is getting ready to go out to work in the fields. Hurry. You have slept like a mouse in a mound of flax."

Talia stretched and turned on her sleeping mat. Her mother was just outside the doorway of their two-room home, in the courtyard where she shared a morning fire with the neighbor women. Talia squinted and blinked and stretched again. She had been dreaming of all the hustle and bustle of the day before—the customers coming into the city in bright clothing. But in her dream there were horses and donkeys and people parading around, and beautiful purple and blue shawls floating down from the tall wall. One shawl had floated right to her feet, and she had breathlessly snatched it up before a horse stepped on it.

The festival was over for another year. Now she would help her farmer father clean up the flax field and get ready for another season next spring. She loved going out into the fields with him. She could see for miles, all the way to the river a morning's walk

7

away. She could sense the wind on her face and in her hair. It made her feel like one of the yellow butterflies that flitted about the flowers and grasses. If she only had that blue shawl in her dream, she could spread it out like wings and fly, really fly.

Baka was toddling around in the courtyard, holding a piece of bread, dropping as many crumbs as he got into his little mouth. Talia stood and wrapped her waistband around her tunic, shaking out her long brown hair and combing it with her fingers as she walked forward into the sunshine. Baka looked up when she reached out her arms to him. He laughed as she lifted him. He kissed her on the mouth, giving her the first taste of breakfast.

Her mother saw and greeted her. "Talia! You are up at last. You must have been far away in your dreams to take so long to get here."

"Oh, Mama! I dreamed of a blue shawl. It floated down to me like the most beautiful cloud in the sky."

"Talia, you are such a dreamer. Come, have some bread, and get ready to go with Papa. He will be back soon from his morning visit with the men."

Talia sat down on the pile of burlap she and Papa would take to the flax field. She squinted in the sunlight and looked around at the people working in the courtyard. Her neighbor was kneading bread; another was bringing water back from the well for cooking; yet another was sweeping the stones in front of her doorway.

Mama kissed the palm of Talia's hand and then placed a warm bun in it. "There now, eat that. Then go wash your face and neck. Bring back a sack of water for your day in the field, please. Take Baka with you. I will have your milk ready for you when you return."

Talia munched on the good bread in her right hand and held onto Baka with her left. He toddled along beside her, babbling and laughing at the neighbors who waved at him as the two of them went around the corner to the well.

There was her cousin Havilah, drawing water and pouring it into a wooden bucket.

"Havilah! Are you going out to the fields today?"

"No, Talia. Mother is sick. I must stay and take care of her."

"Auntie is sick? Mama didn't tell me. I am sorry."

"No, Aunt Hanah probably doesn't know. Mama awakened me during the night. She has a fever, and I am taking this water back to her."

"May I help you? Shall I go with you? I can take Baka back to Mama."

"No, Talia. Thank you. No. I can take care of her."

"But, Havilah—"

"No, Talia. You know you haven't been allowed to see my mother for a while. No! You can't come. I am fine. If I need help, I will send for your mother. Good-bye. I must go. Have a good day in the fields. I will think of you."

"Good-bye, Havilah."

Talia felt sad. It must be hard for her cousin to have lost her brother, to never have known her father, and now to have her mother sick in bed.

The last two years had been so difficult for Havilah's family. When Heth fell from the ladder to the cobblestone pavement, he broke many bones and was knocked unconscious. Aunt Rahab and her family tried to take care of him. When he did not respond after a few days, she called for the priest to come.

He came in his orange robes and lit incense in the room where the frail boy was lying. Everyone was solemn and scared. The priest threw a blue die on the floor and then told Aunt Rahab the gods of Jericho said she had to give a goat and a goose for him to sacrifice to the golden calf at the temple. Then Heth would get well. The priest didn't even look at his broken young body. He just took the bleating goat and squawking goose away. Aunt Rahab watched them go and then returned to sit beside her son, stroking his hand and crying softly.

When he was no better two days later, she called for the priest again. He returned with the acrid incense and the die, which clattered on the floor. This time, he told her she had to pay many shekels. Then the gods would be pleased, and Heth would get better. She sighed deeply, dropped the precious silver pieces into the priest's extended hand and turned away in hope that now her son would get well.

Heth died the next morning.

Talia's father and his brothers Omar and Kedar came to help carry Heth's body out to the burying ground. Talia's grandparents, Saba and Sabta, and the rest of the family all came too. It was such a sad day.

Havilah cried and cried. Their cousin Yakesh, the son of Uncle Kedar and Aunt Selina, was nearly the same age as Heth. He looked so scared. Yakesh wouldn't talk to anyone for days.

Aunt Rahab cried for weeks. Havilah came to be with Talia much of the time. And when Aunt Rahab stopped crying, she got angry. She was angry with the priest, and she was angry with the gods of Jericho who took her goat, her goose, her shekels, and most of all her only son.

Aunt Rahab behaved badly in her time of anger— so badly that Talia's parents wouldn't let her be with her aunt. Sometimes Talia got cross. She couldn't understand. She felt as if she were being punished, and no one would explain things to her.

Talia turned away from her miserable thoughts to pull up a bucket of water from the well. The paving stones held little puddles that entertained Baka while his sister worked.

First she took a scoop from the bucket to a stone bench where she could splash her face and neck. It felt cool and helped wash away the sadness. The blue harvest sky was already pouring out warmth.

Then she plunged her water skin into the bucket and watched the bubbles rise as the skin filled. She pushed the fat end under and saw more bubbles rise. When they stopped, she knew the skin would hold no more, so she put in the wooden stopper and let the water drip off back into the bucket.

She brought one full scoop to her mouth, leaned her head back, and drank deeply. Finally she hefted the heavy bucket, now only a third full, and poured the rest into a trough where passing animals could drink.

Baka was sitting in a puddle, patting his hands in the water, and singing a little song to himself. A sparrow was trying to catch an insect near him. Baka laughed and crawled toward the little bird, scaring it away with his friendliness.

"Come, Baka. Time to go back to Mama."

Baka was reluctant to leave the puddles, but he came cheerfully, waving and laughing at passersby. A goat let him pet it, but his wet hands picked up coarse hairs from the goat's side. Baka rubbed his hand on his tunic to get the hairs off. He scowled and rubbed again. He flicked his fingers and picked at the hairs with his other pudgy hand. Finally Talia laughed at his efforts and rubbed the hairs off with the end of her waistband. Then she took his damp hand and led him home.

Back in their family's little courtyard, Mama had mugs of warm milk ready for her children. It tasted so good to Talia with some of Uncle Omar's golden honey in it.

"Mama, I saw Havilah."

"And is she going to the fields today too?"

"No, Mama. She said Auntie is sick."

"Rahab is sick?"

"Yes. Havilah said she fell ill during the night. I offered to go back with her."

"And?"

"And she said no. She said if she needs help, she will send word to you."

"All right. Thank you, Talia. Baka and I will go visit them later this morning. I will see if Havilah or Rahab need any help."

"Thank you, Mama. Mama?"

"Yes, Talia?"

"May I— May I visit Aunt Rahab when I return?"

"No, Talia. You know you are not permitted to see Aunt Rahab now."

"But, Mama—"

"No. Papa and I have not changed our minds. Until Aunt Rahab changes her ways, you may not go to her inn."

Talia turned away and sulked. She missed her aunt and didn't understand why she wasn't allowed to see her.

When Papa returned from his morning visit, Talia was ready for a day of work.

"Look, Papa. I have water for us and raisin cakes."

"Good, Talia. Let me pick up our tools and the bundle of burlap. There. Off with us now."

"Good-bye, Mama. Good-bye, Baka. Say hello to Aunt Rahab for me."

"Good-bye, my dears. Work well. Return hungry."

Papa laughed and winked at Talia. "She thinks she needs to tell me to return hungry!"

Talia laughed too. The love of her family made bubbles of happiness percolate inside of her. Laughing was so much better than sulking and crying.

Yesterday guests had come in through the wide-open gates of Jericho. Today workers went out through only one side. The other remained shut, guarded by soldiers always on the watch for the possibility of invaders out on the plain.

Talia was glad she lived in such a secure place inside the thick walls. But then one of the soldiers turned and saw her. His eyes locked on her face. His mouth turned up in a strange smile. Talia felt chilled. It didn't look like he was being friendly. Her secure feelings fled away on little goat's feet inside her heart. Her shoulder pushed up against her father's strong arm as they were jostled through the passageway with many other workers.

Donkeys and goats were going out to find pasture and to bring in the last of the harvest. Men and boys joked and nodded to one another. Goats bleated. Donkeys snuffled and shuffled, the wooden wheels of their carts rumbling and rocking the carts as they rolled over the rough road.

Talia recognized a few girls like herself who accompanied their fathers to the fields. Mostly there were boys. Sons were of great value to any man, but when there were none, or none old enough to work, a daughter would have to do. She waved at her friends.

Talia looked up at Papa. He looked down and winked at her. She knew she was more than just a poor substitute for a son. He reached out and squeezed her shoulder tenderly and then turned to nod at a friend.

Beyond the gate the view opened out. No walls. No women tending fires. No houses or market booths. Suddenly there was a patchwork of tended fields, the winter wheat still a silvery green, the alfalfa and oats golden, the fat squash yellow and orange. The fields stretched out for a mile or more and then, as far as Talia's eye could see, the golden plains of Jericho and the silver ribbon of the Jordan. Above that, the pale blue morning sky beyond, above, and all around them.

Though she felt secure inside the walls of Jericho, out here she felt free and—and something more. She never could quite explain it, but she had to admit to herself that inside the walls, there were things that frightened her. Things that were dark. Things that kept her heart from singing.

The priests of their gods frightened her, though she didn't see them often. She had never been to the temple. Papa went there once a year to take a sacrifice to appease the gods: precious silver shekels, if he had any, or a basket of linen or seeds.

Sometimes the priests would go by in a procession in the marketplace, their long orange robes flowing around them. Some of them wore scary masks. Those who didn't wear masks looked almost as scary with their somber faces. Drummers beat out a slow cadence, and the priests droned a strange tune as they passed by.

One evening months before, a neighbor had warned her parents that priests were approaching. Papa and Mama had grabbed her and Baka and pushed them into their room, telling them to be very quiet. One of Talia's friends disappeared that night. Anytime Talia asked her father where she had gone,

Papa was sad and silent. He wouldn't answer her question. He would only hug her tightly for a while and then go back to his work.

Here, outside the walls, a song arose inside her like a lark from their fields of flax. She could feel it bubbling up, lifting away the heaviness, bringing her joy, making her look around for something good. Something—or someone.

At times she could almost hear a voice—a voice, calling her name. And then, just before she could really hear it clearly or see its source, it would get snatched away by the wind. She would try to catch it, but it was gone like the flitting butterflies that danced among her beloved blue flax blossoms.

The five-petaled flowers were long gone now. Only the bulging brown seed balls remained on the thin golden stalks. Most of the stalks had been uprooted and taken to Aunt Rahab's inn to be soaked in cisterns and then laid out to dry on the rooftop for a few months. This winter they would begin the long process of turning the dry stalks into linen fibers.

But enough stalks remained standing to give father and daughter a good day's work of gathering. When they arrived at their field, Papa threw down the pile of burlap scraps they would rip into strips and use to tie the flax stalks into bundles for the return trip to Jericho. She put the water skin and raisin cakes beneath the pile to keep them cool for a while. Then she picked up the rake and took her place just beyond the swing of Papa's strong arms, prepared to gather the uprooted flax into neat piles.

Everywhere she looked, the farmers of Jericho had taken up their tools in their fields. They were separated on different squares of soil, but they were joined in their common labor of bringing in the harvest.

Soon the winter rains would begin, and they would have other work to do within the walls. Today she would enjoy the sun and the wind and her toil alongside her father. And at the end of that day's work, Talia knew Mama would have a warm meal of squash stew waiting for them.

She giggled again to think of her mother's parting words, "Return hungry."

chapter three

Winter in the City

Talia felt blue. The rain was coming down in torrents again, beating against the stone walls of their house. She stood in the doorway, watching. There were rivulets running among the cobblestones, pooling up into puddles.

It was bad enough to be closed inside the walls of Jericho for the cold months following the harvest. But because of the rain, today she would be closed inside their house most of the time too. At least she would have the morning in the shed with Papa, flailing the stiff flax stems.

Talia's thoughts strayed past the gray scene before her to the flax fields beyond the massive wet walls of Jericho. She knew there was only the stubble of brown stems left from their work a few weeks ago, but the new roots would be gladly soaking up this hard rain for the hot months of summer to come.

Movement in the street caught her attention. She watched as Kaleb the baker pushed his cart through the rain. He tried to skirt around the little lakes and jump the street streams with his stubby legs, but he seemed to be getting just as wet from below as he was from above. Talia called to him and waved, but he didn't hear or see her. He was on his rounds to deliver bread to those who didn't make their own like Talia's mama did. Many days he sold his brown bread from his booth in the market; but on rainy days few people were out, so he delivered his good loaves to their doorways.

Bread! Her stomach churned. Time for some food and then work. She turned to grab her waistband from the peg on the wall. She shook out her long brown hair as she tied the sash around her small waist and then bent to roll up her sleeping mat and tuck it in the corner under the lamp stand with the other mats.

"Talia! Where is my little linen lady?"

"Coming, Mama."

Talia stepped out into the covered courtyard where her mother had warm bread and cool water waiting. She was surprised to see Havilah there, sitting on a stool, wrapped in a shawl, and holding Baka.

"Havilah! What are you doing here?"

"Well—I—I slept here last night."

"You slept here last night? Where? At my house?"

"Yes—I—"

"But where? And why?"

Havilah lived in a room in the tower with her mother just two courtyards away. Many times since her brother died, Havilah had eaten meals with Talia. Aunt Rahab had a hard time putting food on the table for the two of them, though of course her family often helped. But Havilah had never spent the night with Talia's family.

"Is something wrong with Aunt Rahab? Did she go away?" Talia was confused.

Mama handed Talia a warm herb drink. "Not so many questions, young lady. Let your cousin answer only what she can."

Baka held out a ball of linen strips Havilah had knotted together for him. He smiled and said, "Boh! Tah-ly! Boh!"

"But, Mama—"

"Talia, Havilah spent the night with us. Papa made a bed for her near us after she came. You were already asleep. Your Aunt Rahab had—had an unexpected guest last evening."

"An unexpected guest?"

"That's enough questions, dear. Eat your bun and get ready to work."

"But . . ."

"Enough questions, Talia." Mama scowled at her.

Some days were harder than others. She looked at Havilah. Havilah returned her look but didn't smile. She pulled her shawl closer around her shoulders and looked away. Talia's thoughts returned to the blue shawl she so longed for, but she set her selfish thoughts aside to focus on Havilah and her hidden sorrow.

Talia sat down beside her. She reached her arms out to Baka, but he drew back and tucked in more closely behind Havilah's shawl. Talia felt rebuffed. Now she was curious and cross. Her warm bun didn't even taste good.

She realized that her bad mood wasn't helping anyone else. She looked at Baka again. He was so cute, even when he pouted. His steps were getting steadier, and he was trying to say her name. She set her bun aside and reached over for him, smiling gently this time. His face lit up as he reached his pudgy hands out for her. "Tah-ly!" he said. Havilah turned to look at her cousin as Baka wiggled away.

"I'm sorry, Havilah," Talia whispered.

Havilah smiled a little and then turned away again.

Talia didn't know what she was sorry about, but she was sorry. The wind picked up and blew a sheet of rain in under the courtyard roof.

It was going to be a long day.

Papa returned from his morning talk with the men. He wrapped a big arm around Talia and another around Havilah, squeezing them tightly. Then he released them and picked up Baka, tossing him high in the air. Mama scolded him. "Yoktan! You might drop my boy. He will look like a broken squash on the cobblestones."

"Ah, Hanah, do not worry. Baka is made of good stuff. You see how he laughs? Laughter is good for us all, is it not, Havilah?" And he squeezed her again as she tried to hide the tears brimming in her pretty brown eyes.

"Come, Talia, we must get to work on our beating. We need to keep your beautiful Mama supplied with thread so she can weave the linen for us, eh? We do not want her to run out of work."

Mama rolled her eyes. Suddenly Papa squeezed her and kissed her heartily on her rosy lips. Mama swatted him with the damp cloth she had been using, leaving a dark mark on his shoulder.

"Come, Havilah, you can help me clean up until your mother sends for you," Mama said to her niece. Havilah picked up Baka and went inside the house. Papa and Talia dashed across the alley to their workshop, shaking off the raindrops and pausing in the doorway to wave to Mama.

Talia turned to Papa with a question burning like a candle in her heart. "Papa?"

"Yes, my little woman?"

"What is wrong? Why did Havilah come? Why won't you and Mama let me visit Aunt Rahab? I miss her!"

"I know, Talia. I know. My sister is . . . my sister has been making some bad choices. Her grief for your cousin Heth made her a little crazy. You must trust your mother and me. It is best you do not visit her now. Let us take care of matters. You just rest your thoughts and let the rain come down. The sun will return. Do you believe it?"

Talia hesitated. "Yes, Papa. I believe it. But it seems so cold now. I am cold."

Papa picked up Talia's shawl and wrapped it around her.

"Papa?"

"Yes?"

"I wish I—"

"What do you wish?"

"I wish I had a shawl of blue. Why can't I?"

"Ah, my daughter, if I could gather the flax blossoms and weave you one, I would. If I could catch the sky and put it in a basket like a ball of yarn, I would. Anything for my favorite girl. But we are not rich. We cannot afford the dyes. You must be content with what you have. Perhaps someday, all will be right. But for now—let me give you a hug."

He wrapped his big arms around her. She would not trade a bundle of blue shawls for the love of her family. She smiled and knew that all was as well as it could be for now.

chapter four

Spring Whispers

The family sleeping room was filled with the soft light of morning. Talia opened one eye and shut it again. The days were getting longer; the sun was rising sooner. The hard winter rains were finally over. She opened both eyes and suddenly remembered: today she and Papa would be returning to the flax fields!

She stretched and turned and tucked her feet up to rise and stretch again. Oh, yes! Today they would go outside the gates into the wide-open spaces. As she reached for her beige tunic, the scent of almond blossoms whirled on the spring winds, whispering the promises of change.

But there had been so many other whisperings recently. She had glimpsed Aunt Rahab in the courtyard whispering to Papa and Mama. Papa and Mama had been whispering to each other. Men had been whispering in the market. Women had been whispering at the well. Talia felt frightened. No one would tell her what the whispers were about. Sometimes she caught a snatch of a whisper—"a horde of people coming."

Was it an army? Did they have horses? Swords? Talia looked around and behind her. No one would answer her questions. The grownups whispered and worried and went on with their work.

One sleepless night she had lain awake thinking about all that. Something was happening. Things were changing somehow. Maybe it was Talia herself. She knew she was growing. Her elbows often got themselves in trouble, and she tripped over her own feet. Mama said she was always falling.

And she spent so much time thinking. She missed Heth. Oh, he had his faults. He was always late for things. And he teased her too much. But he had a dramatic streak and kept Havilah, Yakesh, their other cousins, and her in awe sometimes.

Once during a family gathering, he had grabbed his sister's shawl, wrapped it diagonally across his chest and pretended to be a king's soldier, commanding them all from his bench horse with one of his Aunt Hanah's shuttles, which he slashed around in the air like a sword. Just when he had them all frightened by his antics, he switched the shawl, wrapping it around his shoulders, and walked solemnly along in front of them like a priest, holding his hand out for payment for prayers, keeping his eyes on the cobblestones. Just as quickly, he tied the sash around his waist like an apron, stuffing it with a hank of combed flax to round out his tummy, and got down on his knees to impersonate short chubby Kaleb the baker. He stumped around, handing each cousin a pretend warm bun, patting them on their heads, chucking them under their chins, and wiping his hands on his apron. They laughed and laughed at his cleverness.

Yes, Talia missed her cousin and felt sad for his twin, Havilah. And she was puzzled about angry Aunt

Rahab. When she thought about the priests in their orange robes that swished by her in the market place, she got angry too. Why hadn't they made her cousin better? Why had so much gone wrong?

Maybe the gods of Jericho had no power. Maybe the gods of Jericho didn't even exist. But surely there had to be a god somewhere. Someone she could talk to in the middle of the night when she felt frightened. She thought of the voice she almost heard out in the flax fields sometimes. Who was it? What was it? Was there someone who knew her name? Someone who was calling her?

She didn't know the answers to these things. They ran around in her head like the chaff in the fields whirling in tiny circles with the spring winds.

The fields! She must get ready to go. Papa would be back from his visit with the men, looking for her, and she hadn't even washed or had a morning bun yet.

Talia hurried out to the courtyard where Mama had set up her loom leaning against the wall of their house. She was sending the shuttle flying through the warp, bringing the heddle bars down, returning the shuttle to her right hand. The clay loom weights, tied to the warp ends, danced above the cobblestones as the fabric took shape. Baka was there beside the loom frame, happily playing with his yarn ball, rolling it around Mama's basket of linen threads. He looked up and giggled at his sister. "Tah-ly!" he said.

Mama looked too. "Talia! Well, Miss Sunshine. Did your dreams of a blue shawl tie you in bed?"

Talia laughed. "No, Mama. I slept well—and I smell the almond blossoms! I am so excited that I will be going with Papa to the field today."

"Yes, dear. He will be coming soon. Hurry and get ready."

As Talia walked off to the well to wash up, she stopped to check on a sparrow's nest on a ledge of stone she had noticed many days before. It was tucked up in the roof overhang of a neighbor's house. She knew the eggs had hatched for she could hear the babies peeping when she went by. Straw hung down over the edge, and she could see the mama sparrow sitting on the nest, her wings spread to shield her family from the morning breeze while she waited for the papa sparrow to bring some food. It all looked so cozy up there, though one little rebel had his beak sticking up under his mother's wing. Talia laughed and went on to the well and then back home for her morning bun. By the time Papa returned from talk with the men, Talia was ready to go.

They jostled their way with all the other workers through the crowded gates. Soldiers watched over them. They were lined up inside and outside the gate, watching, watching.

Goats' feet made happy sounds on the gray cobblestones. Donkeys pulled carts of manure out of the city to the fields where the loads would be put to good use. But now the nasty smell made Talia wish they would move along more quickly.

She saw jolly Uncle Omar with his helper Havilah and Uncle Kedar and Cousin Yakesh walking and talking together. She waved to them. They were going to work in Uncle Omar's olive grove and bee yard. And there was Saba, her grandpa, walking with them, tipping his head at her with a broad, wrinkled smile. He must be weary of being shut inside the walls too.

Talia and Papa finally passed through the gates into the wide-open space outside the city walls. The beauty of spring was beyond what Talia had remembered. There before her spread the fields of winter wheat waving in the wind; the olive groves pressing out their bright green leaf buds; and the almond trees all around. Ah, the almond trees in blossom! Their white flowers filled the air with their sweet scent.

Talia inhaled deeply. The beauty squeezed her heart and pushed tears of joy into her eyes. She was so happy to be out here with her Papa.

But then her heart quickened as she remembered the whispers. Her legs suddenly felt weak. She wondered and worried. A horde of people? Where were they? Were they hiding in the almond groves? Was she safe?

She pressed the problem down inside her head, licked her dry lips, and inhaled the almond scent again. Spring was not far along; the almond trees were the wakers of spring.

At her feet alongside the road were wisps of green pushing up between the rocks —star thistle and crowfoot leaves spreading out. They would cheer the travelers later with blue and yellow blossoms.

Soon Papa was telling Talia to set down the water jug and bundle of raisin cakes. Their flax field was a silvery green with the first thin leaves of the plants pushing up through the soil past last year's sprays of brown thin stems. But the star thistle and crowfoot leaves, so welcome along the roadside, were not wanted here. Talia and Papa had their work cut out for them, and she would be glad for the work to keep her warm in the cool breeze as she knelt on the damp ground to pull up the weeds.

As she worked, Talia's worries returned to her. She stood, stretched, and looked around again for this phantom enemy. The whispers, the whispers. Would the walls of Jericho keep its people safe? Would the lazy gods of Jericho do anything to help her family?

She moved closer to Papa as her eyes scanned the trees and the horizon. She blinked hard. She saw nothing unusual. Out in the distance were the big muddy waters of the Jordan River in spring flood. No army of invaders could cross there. At least Jericho was safe from that direction.

Papa interrupted her thoughts. "Talia, you have worked well. What a weed-warrior you are! My best helper. The flax will flourish with your aid. Would you like to take a break? Let's have some water and a raisin cake, eh?"

They sat down on a big rock, being careful not to crush the narcissus blades. The water felt cool and good, sliding down her throat. The day had warmed, though it was not yet noontime. Talia removed her waistband, pulled her damp hair away from her neck, and tied it back.

As they ate their raisin cakes, Talia thought perhaps this would be a good time to tell her father of her troubled thoughts.

"Papa?"

"Yes, Talia? What is it that you are thinking about so hard?"

"Papa, I love the flax field. I love the wind in my hair. But, Papa?"

"Yes, Talia. I am listening, my linen lady."

"Sometimes I am afraid."

"What are you afraid of, Talia? I am here."

"Yes, Papa, but sometimes I am afraid . . . that the flax fields will go away . . . that the wind will stop blowing . . . that, that you will go away, Papa."

"Little blossom, I am not going to go away."

"But, Papa, what if you do? What if someone takes you away?"

"Oh, Talia, no one is going to take me away!" her father reassured her.

"People say there is an enemy coming—an army. Papa, I am afraid."

Papa looked out across the fields for a moment, leaning on his hoe. He sighed heavily. Then he bent down and put his hand on Talia's shoulder and looked her straight in the eye. He tucked his finger under her trembling chin and spoke softly.

"Talia, the walls of Jericho are big and strong. They will keep us safe. And we have to believe that the gods of Jericho are watching over us."

"But, Papa . . ." Tears trickled down Talia's cheeks. She swallowed hard and went on, "But, Papa, I don't believe in the gods of Jericho."

She shook her small fist in anger and then leaned against her father's big shoulder and crumpled into choking sobs.

Papa held Talia tightly. Then something strange happened. He began to talk out loud in a shaky voice, but not to her; she didn't think he was talking to her. Talia quieted her crying so she could hear him.

"Lord, help us. God above all gods, hear my voice. I have heard yours many times out here. Please help my family. Lord above all lords, work wonders. We beg of your most high honor—hear me. I cry out to you. Rescue us."

Talia tilted her head back. Papa had heard the voice too! Tears were trickling down his brown face. She had never seen him cry.

Just then in the distance trumpets sounded. Papa and Talia looked toward the wall of the city and then at each other.

"The warning sound of danger! We must return. Quickly, Talia. Gather up your tools."

Talia's heart jumped into her throat. Danger. She could hear it in the trumpets. She could hear it in Papa's urgency. She could feel it in the air. As they gathered their few tools and the remainder of their lunch and water jug, they glanced around them. All the workers were hurrying to gather their belongings. Some were already out on the road. Uncle Omar, Uncle Kedar, and Cousin Yakesh were rushing toward them, poor Saba trying to keep up, being steadied by sweet Havilah at his side.

And far out in the distance there was a dark mass of movement. Talia strained her eyes to see.

It was a host of people on the near side of the Jordan River, slowly moving toward Jericho, slowly moving toward them.

chapter five

Under Oath

Talia was breathless and thirsty when she and Papa finally cleared the gates of Jericho. People were pushing and pressing to get in, panic on their faces. Everyone was talking, talking. Fear was in the air. So were feathers! Geese and ducks were fluttering and flying around, trying to stay out of the rush and roar of the returning workers.

Talia caught snatches of people's questions and comments as Papa guided her home.

"Our soldiers are well-trained for battle."

"There must be a million of them coming."

"The walls will keep us safe."

"But what if—"

"Do we have enough food and water for a siege?"

Papa nodded somberly to his brothers Omar and Kedar as they parted ways for the time being.

Talia's shoulders felt tight. "Papa, Papa, what is happening?"

"Hush, Talia. We must get home to Mama and Baka and away from all this noise."

As they turned the corner to their courtyard, they saw Mama and Baka watching and waiting for them. Baka ran forward saying, "Horsies, Taly! Baka saw horsies!" He was clutching a bunch of goose feathers.

Mama rushed up to Papa and embraced him and then turned to Talia and hugged her. Mama always smelled of the cooking fire and laundry soap and hard work. "I was worried! I thank the gods you have returned. I heard rumors—"

"Hanah, hush. Do not worry the children. We will hear many rumors. Hush now. Let us go inside. Talia is tired."

Papa scooped up Baka and guided them all into the main room of their home. Mama quickly set the table with fresh greens. A pot of stew was steaming on the fire out in the courtyard for their evening meal. Talia unpacked the raisin cakes she and Papa had not eaten.

Then she slumped into her chair and started to cry. She was tired and relieved to be home again and so full of questions. Baka leaned over and patted her shoulder with his little hand.

"Taly cry?" he asked.

Mama said with a shaky voice, "Talia, stop crying, dear. Don't upset Baka."

Talia looked up and saw Mama's wet eyes. They strengthened each other with a long look and took big breaths to control themselves.

"That's my girls. Now, let's eat. We will talk later." Papa sat down at his place.

After the strained silence of a late midday meal, Mama sent Talia off to the coolness of the inner room to play quietly with Baka and to rest. Mama said she would take care of the table and resume her other work. Papa left to talk with the men in the marketplace.

Baka had his fistful of feathers from the courtyard. Talia counted them for him and put them in a little pot beside their sleeping mat. Then she sang him a funny song and watched him fall asleep smiling.

Talia's head hurt. A day that had started with such anticipation had turned suddenly to one of fear. She was glad at least that she got outside the walls of Jericho to see the almond trees in bloom. And to talk with Papa.

Why was so much good mixed up with so much bad? Why couldn't a day just be all good? Why did she have to feel afraid? Why did she have to wonder, wonder all the time? Wasn't there anyone who could tell her the answers to her questions? Did the grownups know? If they did, why wouldn't they tell her? And if even they didn't know—who did? She dozed off as these questions whirled inside her head.

Talia awakened with Baka curled up beside her, his damp head resting on her arm. She carefully lifted his head and pulled her arm away. She watched her brother. Baka moaned, smacked his little lips, sighed, and went back to sleep. She turned over and lay on the blanket in the dim light.

Outside in the courtyard, Talia heard muffled voices. Papa! He was back from the marketplace and was talking quietly to Mama. Talia jumped up, retied her sash, and ran out to the courtyard, which was glowing softly in the late day sun.

"Papa! What is happening?"

Mama said, "Shh, Talia. Don't be rude. You must not burst into our conversation."

"I'm sorry, Mama. I'm sorry, Papa. But—"

"No, Talia. You must wait quietly until you are invited into the talk."

Talia threw a desperate look at Papa.

"Hanah. Let me talk with Talia. She is so concerned."

Mama shrugged her shoulders and turned to put more wood on the fire. Papa pulled Talia to his side.

"I've been in the marketplace. This is what I know. There is a large group of people coming, and they have crossed the Jordan River."

Talia said, "I saw all those people on this side of the river when I was with you. But . . . they crossed? Crossed the Jordan? That's where they came from? How could they cross? It is in flood! I saw it this morning!"

"They were completing their crossing, even as you saw them."

"But . . ."

"I know. It is hard to believe. They seem to have some sort of magic—or their god—in a box they carry with them."

"A box?"

"I am told our spies saw them—priests carrying a box with poles. When they stepped into the edge of the river, the waters parted."

"The waters parted? How?"

"No one knows how. It seems to be some kind of powerful sorcery. The river stopped flowing and piled up in heaps of water, and the priests stood in the middle while the people hurried and walked across."

"Papa, I can't believe it. How can this be?"

"No one knows how this can be. But we know that the hand of their god is mighty, and we are in fear of them and their god."

"But if their god can do this, . . . their god can do anything!"

"You are right, Talia. It appears that their god *can* do anything."

"But what will happen? What will we do? Will there be a big battle? Where will we go?"

"The men say our king has ordered our soldiers to be on the ready. He knows our walls will hold and that the invaders cannot succeed. Far fewer than half of them are equipped for battle. For now our army will watch and see what this people will do."

"But—our fields. Our plantings. The blue flax blossoms. What will we do?"

"Nothing for now. The city is shut up tightly. We must work here and wait and watch as well."

"But, Papa, what if—"

"Talia, there is more. I have told you what I have heard in the marketplace. But there is another viewpoint."

"Another viewpoint?" Talia glanced up and saw her mother watching them intently. Papa nodded at her. "Let's step inside the house to talk."

Mama smiled and waved at a neighbor as Papa and Talia sat down at the table. She came in and brought cups of water for them all. The cool spring morning had turned warm late in the day.

Papa took a deep breath and went on. "The other viewpoint is your Aunt Rahab's. Talia, you must tell no one this."

"Papa, I won't. But what does Aunt Rahab have to do with this?"

"She—she harbored guests at her inn several weeks ago."

"But she often does."

"Yes, Talia. But these two men were . . ."

"Were what, Papa?"

"Talia, you must tell no one."

"I won't, Papa! But what? What were the men? Who were they?"

"Talia, these men were spies."

"Spies? Why, Papa? From where? Are they dangerous? Papa, are we safe?" Talia scooted closer on the bench to her mother. Mama wiped her hands, touched Talia's shoulder, and stroked her daughter's long hair.

"Talia, the men were from this people who crossed the river today. They say they are the people of God, coming to conquer this land."

"The people of God? What do you mean?"

"They told Rahab that the god they worship is the God in heaven above and on earth beneath. He is greater than any god we know. And He has been working wonders for His people!"

"Wonders?"

"They came from Egypt where they had been kept as slaves. And their God dried up the water of the Red Sea so they could escape from the Egyptian army. He helped them destroy the kings of the Amorites. And now they have crossed our own Jordan River in spring flood. Nothing seems to stop them."

"Oh, Papa, what will happen to us?"

"Here is the good news, Talia. Aunt Rahab has changed her ways. She was courageous in talking to them. She was kind to them, and she believes in their God. She has received an oath."

"An oath?"

"Yes, a solemn promise that can't be broken. Aunt Rahab hid the spies and helped them to escape in exchange for a promise that they would spare her life and those of her whole family."

Just then Baka appeared in the doorway, rubbing his eyes with his chubby hand. His hair was damp and mashed against his head from his long nap. Mama scooped him up and took him out to the courtyard to hold him in her lap and give him a drink while Papa and Talia continued to talk quietly.

"Our whole family? Us, Papa? What did they say?"

"They said that if she told no one about their business, and if she had her family gathered inside her house when they returned, and if she had a sign outside her window, then they would deal kindly with her."

"What kind of a sign, Papa?"

"A scarlet cord."

Talia sat quietly and thought about all this. She fidgeted with her sash, pulling the ends of the frayed threads, twisting them around her fingers. She didn't know how long she sat like this. She was startled when her father laid his hand on her shoulder and broke into her thoughts.

"Talia? What are you thinking?"

She started to cry. She didn't know how to talk about her fears. So she said, "I am thinking about my blue shawl. I would like to have a blue shawl to wrap around me."

"Let me wrap my arms around you. Here, Talia, pretend I am your blue shawl." He picked her up in his brawny arms and then whispered, "Do you understand why it is important for you to tell no one about our talk?"

"Yes, Papa, I understand. I will tell no one."

"Good. I am going now to the marketplace to confer with your uncles and see what is happening."

"Thank you, Papa. Thank you for everything—for talking to me and helping me to understand. Thank you for being better than a blue shawl to me."

Papa smiled, patted her cheek, and went out.

Talia stepped into the late afternoon light and wrapped her arms around her little brother. He laughed and snuggled up to her, handing her another bouquet of feathers.

Mama smiled too.

chapter six

A Special Visitor

Talia felt trapped. It had been four weeks since she and Papa had made their spring venture out into the beautiful fields and groves of trees beyond the gates of Jericho. Now the gates remained tightly shut. Soldiers milled around the marketplace by day; horses clopped by in the alleys at night. Tension was so thick you could tear it like a loaf of Mama's brown bread. But the bread was being parceled out. No one knew how long the gates would remain closed. Perhaps their grain would have to be rationed.

One clear night after a refreshing spring rain, Talia rose quietly from her sleeping mat and stepped out into the courtyard. She was startled by a sudden glimpse of beauty: the full moon was reflected in a pool of water caught in the cobblestones. Talia drew in her breath and slowly exhaled. She looked cautiously into the shining darkness and then stepped out into the moonlight. She gazed up at the stars and moon, suspended just above the massive stone wall behind her.

She thought about the moonlight spilling out onto their field beyond the wall. How lovely the flax blossoms must be in the bright night. She wished she could go out to see them. She wished she could work beside Papa, pulling the weeds, watching the butterflies, swatting the flies, sitting on a warm rock to eat the raisin cakes and drink from the water bag. The field must need them. The gray-green stems would be as high as Baka's chest by now, and no one was there to tend to them, to see their delicate cone-shaped blue buds, to pull the weeds away so they could stretch out and grow.

The clip-clop of a horse and its soldier on patrol around the next building sent her bare feet skittering back inside. She tucked them in under the light linen cover, pulled it up over Baka's shoulder, and sighed in the darkness. She could yearn all she wanted to go out to the flax field, but perhaps it would be better to talk to Aunt Rahab's God.

She wished she knew how. The priests of Jericho chanted their prayers to the gods as they burned the sacrifices. No one else talked to those gods. Papa had talked directly to one he had called "Lord of all lords" and "God of all gods." Could she get into trouble calling on a God she didn't know? But she felt she did know Him. She felt He knew her.

As she thought and felt and wondered these things, she dozed off into a deep slumber.

In the bright light of late morning, Talia awakened to the cool touch of her mother's hand on her forehead.

"Talia, dear. Are you all right? You have been moaning, and you slept so late."

Talia turned over and squinted. Her head throbbed and her voice caught in her sore throat. Her chest ached, and so did her knees and elbows.

"Mama. I am sick. How did I get sick? I was well last night."

"I don't know, Talia. But there has been much sickness going on in Jericho. The stress and strain of being shut in is wearing on people."

"Mama, my head hurts. My throat hurts."

"You have a fever, sweet one. I will make you a hot drink of healing herbs and bring you some bread."

"I don't want to eat."

"Just lie here and rest. I will come back."

Talia dozed and awakened again to the buzz of voices in the courtyard. Baka toddled in, carrying his yarn ball.

"Taly pway boh?"

"No, Baka. I can't play ball. Sissy is sick."

"Sissy sick?"

"Yes. My head hurts. My legs hurt." A tear trickled down her hot cheek.

Baka stooped down and looked at his sister, his small round face serious. He patted her arm and pulled up the cover for her. Then he walked back out, leaving his yarn ball beside the bouquet of goose feathers.

Soon Mama returned with a steaming mug. It smelled like mint. Baka was beside her, holding her skirt, and peering out at Talia. He hadn't seen her like this before.

"Can you sit up a bit, Talia? Here, drink this. It will soothe your throat and chase your fever away. Just take a sip. Good."

The hot herbs did soothe her throat. Talia took several careful sips before she lay back down and let her mother tuck her in.

She slept again, but the fever brought bad dreams. She saw monstrous men with sharp talons instead of fingers, beating on the walls of Jericho, trying to climb over them. The sky grew dark, and large birds swooped down into the streets and alleys, dropping dirty rags everywhere. The rags hit the cobblestones and turned into rats, running into houses, chewing on people's feet.

Talia awakened with a jerk, pulling her feet away from the sharp teeth of an imaginary rat. "Mama! Papa!"

Mama ran back into the room. "Talia. Are you all right?"

"I had horrible dreams, Mama. Big men were coming over the walls; rats were running everywhere and chewing, chewing."

"Shh, quiet, Talia. You will frighten Baka. Let me feel your head."

Mama slid one soft hand behind Talia's neck; the other pushed her damp hair away from her forehead. That felt so good, so soothing.

"Your fever has broken. You should feel a bit better soon. I want you to rest today. But Aunt Rahab has come with news. She wants to talk to you."

"Aunt Rahab? I haven't seen her in so long! Can she come in now?"

"Shh, be still. Don't get excited. Yes, she is in the courtyard, talking to Papa. I will tell her you are ready for her to come in, but don't get worked up, Talia, dear. You need to rest and get well quickly."

"Get well quickly, Mama? Why?"

"Rahab will tell you. Lie back and close your eyes. She will be in shortly."

Mama stood, and then stooped again to straighten Talia's blanket and brush her hair away from her face.

She smiled and walked away with soft footsteps, stirring Baka's bouquet of feathers beside the sleeping mat. The yarn ball rolled away.

Talia closed her eyes.

Aunt Rahab leaned in the doorway and called softly to her sleeping niece, "Talia. Talia. May I come in?"

Talia's eyes popped open, and she sat up in bed. "Aunt Rahab! Aunt Rahab, I'm so glad to see you." She pressed her hand to her mouth to suppress a sob and then offered both hands to receive her aunt's warm embrace. "Oh, Aunt Rahab. I've missed you."

"I've missed you, too, dear. How are you feeling?" Aunt Rahab loosened Talia's grip and pushed her back gently to look at her. She stroked her niece's forehead and wiped tears away from Talia's pale face.

Talia realized she still felt quite achy and weak. She lay back down but placed her hands in her aunt's lap. "Why couldn't I see you, Aunt Rahab? Where have you been?"

A motion in the doorway caught their attention. Baka had walked in, carrying a bun. He laughed when he saw his sister and aunt.

A voice from the courtyard scolded, "Baka! Come back here! I told you to leave your sister alone."

Baka turned toward the voice, and then looked at Talia again. "Taly," he said and extended his bun toward her. He smiled at Aunt Rahab.

"Baka!" Mama stepped into the room. Baka frowned and turned in fear. He lost his balance, fell with his little legs tangled up, and dropped his bun. He began to cry.

Mama scolded again. "Baka, I told you to stay in the courtyard with me. You have disobeyed."

Baka cried harder and reached his arms up to his mother. She bent down and picked him up, hugging him to her shoulder. She kissed the top of his head and apologized to her sister-in-law and daughter. As she walked back out with her roly-poly rebel, they heard her telling Baka that he must listen and obey.

Aunt Rahab's eyes laughed quietly. "Do you see, Talia? I was like your little brother. After Heth died, I was so angry. I turned away from the gods of Jericho and many of the things I believed in. I went my own way."

"I'm sorry you were so angry, Auntie. I was mad too. I miss Heth. I miss him a lot. And I've missed you."

"Yes, Talia. I'm so sorry."

"But what happened, Aunt Rahab? How did you change?"

"Well, in my quiet moments I began to hear a voice. It seemed as if someone was calling my name."

"A voice, Aunt Rahab? I've heard a voice too. I have! Oh, Aunt Rahab, who is it?" Talia sat up on her knees and stared hard into her aunt's face.

"I'm not at all sure, Talia. But I felt as if someone lifted me up and turned me around. I . . . I felt cared for . . . and called.

"Through my business at the inn, I heard rumors that a people were on the move from the southeast and that they claimed to have a god who moved with them. Their god was doing miracles for them."

"But do you believe it? Are you afraid?"

"Well, I was afraid. But then a strange thing happened."

"What? The spies?" Talia clapped her hands together quietly.

"Yes. The spies. Two men. They came needing information, and I chose to help them."

"Why? Why did you?"

"They treated me respectfully, and they were kind. They spoke of their God. They said He is the only true God, the Creator of all people."

"Do you believe them?"

"Yes, Talia, I do. I believe their Lord is the God in heaven above and on earth beneath. Talia, I believe He is the true God of Jericho."

"But, Aunt Rahab, will the gods be angry at us if we say these things?"

"Talia, I don't believe the gods of Jericho even exist."

Talia thought for a moment, and then said, "Papa told me . . ."

"What did Papa tell you?"

"He told me that you hid the spies and helped them to escape in exchange for a promise."

"That's right, Talia. They promised that they would spare my life and all of my family who are in my house."

"Is the sign in your window, Aunt Rahab? Papa said there is a sign. The scarlet cord?"

"Yes, dear, it is."

"Will they see it? Will they rescue us?"

"Talia, I believe their God is watching over us, and we will be rescued. I believe that with all my heart."

"Oh, Aunt Rahab. I do too!"

Aunt Rahab kissed Talia's forehead and then gently tucked her in. "You need to rest, Talia. Get some sleep now, and do not worry."

Talia grasped her aunt's hand then released it and snuggled under her blanket. As Aunt Rahab headed quietly toward the doorway, Talia suddenly asked, "Aunt Rahab, can Havilah come visit me?"

"Maybe in a day or two when you are much better. Now you must rest."

Talia smiled, closed her eyes, and slept.

chapter seven

Inside the Tower

Talia felt well and strong after several days. She was comforted by the talks with her papa and her aunt and gladdened by Havilah's visits. But the days stretched out: long days of being inside the gates, days of being careful how much they ate, days of people looking worried and afraid.

Then came a change, a frightening change. News spread like dragonflies flashing in the flax field that the invaders were on the move. They were coming in a procession. Four of their men carried the box that held their god. Seven more men marched in front of them, blowing rams' horns. Behind the box were armed soldiers, many of them, marching, marching, marching toward Jericho.

Papa called his family together. "We must get ready to go to Rahab's," he said in a calm voice. "Talia, gather sleeping mats, and then get Baka. Hanah, we should take bread and water. Rahab has stored up some provisions, but we must help. Quickly, everyone.

I will go to make sure the rest of our family is getting ready."

Jericho suddenly seemed like a swarm of bees in the summer—everyone buzzing, hurrying about in crazy circles. Talia felt excited and scared. Mama dashed off to fill their water sacks at the well while Talia had Baka help her roll up their mats. Her head felt like a swarm of bees too, with so many questions flying around. What would happen? Would these priests and soldiers hurt them? She remembered her terrible dream. Did these strange people have claws that would help them crawl up the strong walls of Jericho? How long would her family have to stay in Aunt Rahab's tower? Would their new God really protect them?

Baka grunted as he rolled up his sleeping mat. "Taly, Baka work!" he said proudly. Talia loved how her brother was becoming a little worker. She patted his head and placed the lopsided roll with the others in a pile by the doorway. She spotted her mother hurrying back from the well, the water bags dripping and leaving a thin dark trail on the cobblestones behind her. She spotted Papa too, coming around the corner from another alley. She grabbed her shawl and Baka's hand and hurried out to hear the news.

"Omar is helping Saba and Sabta gather their things," Papa reported, a bit out of breath. "They will be along shortly. We must go on and see if Rahab needs help."

Talia wrapped her shawl around her waist and picked up two of the mats. They were awkward to carry. Mama had a large linen bundle with bread in one arm; she reached for Baka's hand with her other. Papa gathered the bigger mats and the bags of water.

It was only three short alleys and one long street to the stairs that led to Aunt Rahab's guesthouse in the wall, but the stairs—there were many of them! Talia counted them for a while, but she also had to concentrate on keeping up with Mama, who had shifted her bundle of bread and gathered up Baka. His chubby legs were too short for all these stairs.

"Twenty-nine, thirty, thirty-one," she continued to count and then shifted her load of mats and tried to get her breath. When she stopped, she could hear the trumpets blowing beyond the walls, getting closer. That frightened her. She hurried to catch up with Mama, tears suddenly stinging her eyes. She thought she saw someone coming up behind her in the dark stairwell, but when she turned to look, she realized it was only her own shadow. She must be brave. Papa and Aunt Rahab said their new God would deliver them. She must believe that.

It was cool and dark inside Aunt Rahab's house. Several family members were already there. A cousin helped with the mats, finding a place along the wall to stack them with their other belongings. Papa put a small cloth bag on top of the bread, away from the water bags. Talia looked at him quizzically.

He smiled and whispered, "Flax seeds."

Flax seeds. Papa was truly prepared to leave Jericho. To leave their home, their neighbors, their field, their work. She looked at him again, her lips quivering. He placed his hand on her shoulder and said, "It's okay, Talia. We will be all right. The Lord above all lords has promised to preserve us."

The sound of the trumpeting rams' horns had grown faint. Talia looked around the room. There was Aunt Rahab, greeting her family, hugging and helping them. There was Havilah, crossing the room toward her.

And there in the window was a scarlet cord.

Uncle Omar arrived with Saba and Sabta. His merry eyes twinkled at his nieces. He winked at Talia. The grandparents were weary from the long climb up the staircase. Aunt Rahab settled them comfortably in chairs in a corner away from the gathering group. It was almost like a holiday, except that there was hushed talk instead of loud laughter. Talia and Havilah pressed up against each other. The little room was crowded with family and the few possessions they brought with them.

"Where is Aunt Selina?" Talia asked her cousin.

"I don't know. I haven't seen her or Uncle Kedar."

"Yakesh?"

"No, not Yakesh either." Havilah shook her head sadly.

The day passed slowly, everyone wondering silently what would happen. The sound of the horns had faded away. Uncle Omar kept watch at the high window in the wall. His taller brother Yoktan could see out of it, but he had to stand on a bench. He reported that the soldiers had left. No one knew when they would return.

Evening came. The room darkened, but Aunt Rahab lit no lamps. Each family unit gathered to eat some bread and cheese or dates in the dusk, and then settled on their sleeping mats in the crowded room. They could have moved into other guest rooms, but it felt more secure to be together in one place.

Morning came—and the sound of the trumpets approaching: "*Ta-ruah, ta-ruah,*" they shrilled over and over. Talia awakened, wondering where she was, and then felt the tension in the room before she even recognized the eerie sound coming through the window. Aunt Rahab had instructed everyone to be silent whenever they heard the rams' horns. Baka cried.

Mama quieted him, distracting him with a scrap of linen she waved around like a bird. Finally he laughed and tried to grab it. She hid it behind her back and he jumped to get it. Papa looked at her sharply, and she shushed their son again.

Uncle Omar was at his station by the window, Papa beside him, watching and listening. As each person awoke, he rose and looked around and stretched, and then silently rolled up his sleeping mat and set it in a pile. All was quiet except for the disturbing sounds of the rams' horns. Talia wished she could see out the window, but she was too short. She and her cousin stood beside each other against the wall of the room.

The haunting sound of horns faded as the marching men moved around the mighty wall of Jericho. Aunt Rahab and Mama with Baka in her arms walked around the room, silently offering bread to everyone. No one seemed to have an appetite.

Uncle Omar and Papa craned their necks to see what was happening. They continued to watch until all was quiet. Finally Uncle Omar stepped off the bench. Papa turned to look at everyone and said, "They have gone away again."

There was a big sigh of relief. Havilah and Talia collapsed on the pile of sleeping mats and closed their eyes. Suddenly they felt hungry. They found the basket of bread and plundered it, passing it around for their cousins to join in while the grownups talked in hushed tones.

The whole rest of the day stretched before them. Aunt Rahab occupied the girls with sweeping the floors, but she wouldn't let them go out on the rooftop or down the stairs. She said it was important for them to stay in her house.

Evening came. The room darkened, but again no lamps were lit. Everyone ate quietly and settled down for another night in the crowded room. This time Talia and Havilah were allowed to put their sleeping mats next to each other. Baka squeezed between them. Soon the gentle sounds of sleeping people filled the room, and Talia dropped off to sleep as well.

Sometime during the night, she awakened. The sweet sounds of sleep still filled the darkness, but the sweetness seeped away as Talia thought again of some who were missing—her cousin Yakesh, Papa's sister Selina, and her husband Kedar. Where were they? Why weren't they sleeping here with Aunt Rahab's whole family? Talia had been so worried about other things for three days that she hadn't thought of them. She felt bad to have forgotten them. She turned on her side and drifted back to sleep.

Morning came and the sound of the trumpets again. It was unpleasant and unsettling to hear only them and no other sound from down on the plain— no shouting, no jeering. Just the muffled tramping of many feet and the horns. But Rahab's family could hear shouting from somewhere near her window. Papa had a limited view; he suspected that there might be city soldiers on the wall, taunting the men below them.

The sounds awakened Talia. She turned on her mat and then remembered her missing family members. Baka cried. Mama comforted him.

When the unwelcome sounds of stomping feet and blowing horns had faded, Talia sought out her father to ask him about Yakesh and his parents. Papa bent down to look in her face sadly and then hugged her to him with a big sigh.

"What is it, Papa? Why don't you answer me?"

"Sometimes there are no words, Talia. I tried to persuade my sister to come, but she refused. I wonder if she does not understand the danger or if she thinks there is no hope. I don't know. She and Kedar simply would not come."

"But Papa, Yakesh is my friend. I love Aunt Selina and Uncle Kedar. I want them to be here with us."

"I know, Talia. Your Mama and I do too."

"Can't we do anything, Papa? Can't we go and plead with them?"

"No, Talia. We cannot leave this place. We must stay here."

"But, Papa—"

"No, Talia! We cannot do anything."

Papa thought a moment. "Yes, yes, there is something we can do. Perhaps we could pray. Perhaps we could talk to the One who is our Refuge."

"Oh, yes, Papa! Let's talk to Him."

Papa grasped his daughter's cold hands in his big warm ones, closed his eyes, and began to talk. "Lord of all lords, You have heard our prayer for help. You have provided a place of refuge and hope for our family. We thank you, great and powerful God.

"But not all are here. Your Most High Honor, we beg of You, turn the hearts of my sister's family to You. Let them hear Your voice as we have. Rescue them, O Mighty One. I cry out to You. Spare them."

Papa loosened his grasp. Talia looked up at him, her eyes shining with tears. Papa picked her up in a big hug, then set her down with a pat on the head and turned to confer with Uncle Omar again.

The day passed slowly. Aunt Rahab set Havilah and Talia to work, weaving sashes from linen thread she had in a basket. That made the time go much more quickly, and Baka enjoyed playing with a yarn ball they made for him.

Three more days passed, the same as the first three, except that their curiosity and concern about the strange army grew while their stockpile of water and food diminished. Uncle Omar, Papa, Sabta, and Aunt Rahab spent many hours together near the scarlet cord, whispering and shaking their heads solemnly.

That evening of the sixth day, before Aunt Rahab and Mama passed out the dinner rations, Uncle Omar addressed the weary group:

"First, we want to thank our sister Rahab for providing this place of refuge for us. We are all indebted to her for her courage in speaking with the spies of the invading army and securing their help in exchange for hers. She has told us that we must remain here together until the danger is clearly past. This is what she has promised the spies who were here and who in turn solemnly made an oath to rescue any of her family who would be with her if—when—the walls of Jericho are breached.

"But we do not know what this strange army is doing. We have never before faced this threat. However, we face a further threat. Our rations are running low. We need water and grain. If the army continues to march around Jericho day after day, we could starve to death.

"There is great danger in leaving this room. We have consulted with Rahab, and she is gravely concerned. The spies told her that they are responsible to deliver only those who are here in her house with her. If anyone leaves, he is on his own. He may perish with no promise of protection."

"We have carefully weighed these dangers and have decided that tomorrow after the army has passed by and gone away again, Yoktan will go down out of the tower to resupply us all."

Talia shot a glance at her papa. She implored him with her eyes to take her with him. He only nodded slightly, raising a hand to silence her.

Everyone solemnly settled onto his or her mat as dusk approached. Not knowing what would happen, not knowing when it would happen was so hard. Talia patted Baka's back to help him quiet down for sleep; then she and Havilah whispered for a while and nodded off too.

Before dawn on the morning of the seventh day, Talia arose and quietly begged Papa to let her and Havilah go with him. He talked to Hanah and Rahab. The women shook their heads and looked several times at the sleepy girls. Papa seemed to prevail upon them. Finally he turned and stepped over to his daughter and niece.

"Mama and Aunt Rahab reluctantly agree that you may accompany me. You will both actually be a big help to carry things back. We must do everything in great haste in order to return to the safety of our refuge. As soon as the rams' horns sound this morning, we will go."

Even as he said this, the horns could be heard— the signal that the army was making its single circle around the city. It was not long before Papa, Havilah, and Talia were out the door and headed down the dark stairway. Fresh air flowed up into their faces as they descended, and then light and street sounds guided them to the bottom.

The trio hesitated as they stood there in the cobblestone courtyard, surprised at how deserted it seemed and curious at the sound of distant shouting and chanting. Some women and children were busy with morning chores, but no merchants or other men were in sight.

The distant shouting drew their attention. Talia stood between Havilah and Papa, gazing upward. The orange flags snapped in the spring breeze, high above the mighty stone walls of Jericho. Talia tilted her head back to look at them, hanging on to the ends of her shawl as it slipped down her shoulders.

She remembered how proud she had been only a few months ago of the stone walls of Jericho. She had thought that no army could get past or over them. She had felt safe. But now she knew that the strong God they had learned to talk to—Aunt Rahab's God—was their refuge, their place of safety. An army might get past the mighty gates of Jericho, but this Lord of lords would take care of them.

The shouting and chanting came from the top of the wall as Papa had suspected from inside the tower. But it wasn't just soldiers. It looked like every man and boy in Jericho was up there! They were shaking their fists, laughing and jeering. Talia looked at Havilah in shocked surprise. The men of Jericho were taunting the strange army with their rams' horns and the odd box they carried with them in the middle of their procession.

Talia looked up at Papa. He, too, was surprised. He shook his head in disbelief.

Then came the next surprise of the morning: the sound of the rams' horns again! It seemed to silence the men on the wall momentarily as their heads turned to follow the procession far below them. The sound of the horns had not disappeared as it had for six days. It was returning loud and strong.

Talia felt terribly frightened. Papa took her hand. He looked soberly at her and her cousin. "Something has changed. This army has not gone away. It seems to be making a second circle around the wall."

"What does that mean, Papa?"

"I don't know, Talia. But we truly must hurry. I will head to our home for the grain. You girls can run to the well to fill the water sacks while I load up my pack with all I can find. Hurry. I will meet you back here as soon as possible."

Then all three looked up again at the wall. The men had resumed their shouting. Snatches of their chanting fell down to their ears.

"Ha-ha, this puny army will march and play again!"

"Go ahead. Play your children's games."

"We stand strong and safe above you!"

"Jericho, Jericho! Mighty, mighty Jericho!"

"Hurry, girls. Go." Papa squeezed Talia's shoulder and turned up the alley toward their home.

Havilah grabbed Talia's hand and practically dragged her away from the courtyard, heading in the opposite direction. They each carried three empty water sacks that slapped against their tunics as they ran. The sounds of the horns and the shouting rang in Talia's head as she tried to keep pace with Havilah's longer legs.

She was breathing hard by the time they slowed in the avenue of merchants; it was nearly deserted. Kaleb's bread oven was steaming, but the baker was nowhere to be seen. How glad Talia would have been of a fresh bun and a grin of greeting from her big friend. Could he be with the other men on top of the wall?

Havilah tugged on her hand again. Talia tied her shawl around her waist. They raced to pull up a bucket of water from the well. The paving stones held little puddles where pigeons tapped and scratched for remnants of food. The bucket of water splashed. The birds scattered, scolded the girls, and then came back to pick at bugs. Talia kept thinking of the words of the spies. *If anyone leaves, he is on his own. He may perish with no promise of protection.* Her throat tightened. She knew she must hurry, but her hands and feet felt like stones. She shook her head hard and began to move again. The splashing water felt cool and good on Talia's feet; it helped wash away her worries.

She plunged her water skin into the bucket and watched the bubbles rise as she had so many times before. She pushed the fat end under and saw more bubbles rise. When they stopped, she put in the wooden plug and let the water drip off back into the bucket. Havilah plunged one of her water skins into the half-empty bucket while Talia tended to her first one.

She longed to drink deeply of this fresh cool water, but she knew she must hurry for the sake of the others—and for her own sake. *He may perish. He may perish,* echoed in her head. She took in a big breath and tried to relax a little.

She scooped a handful of water to her lips, and then put her full sack on the stone bench. When Havilah lifted her water skin to seal it, Talia hefted the nearly empty bucket and lowered it into the well. She helped Havilah pull it up this time; they filled their second sacks, lowered the bucket a third time, and filled once more.

Havilah poured the rest into the animal trough. A goat had just come looking for a drink. Talia quickly scratched him between his little pointy horns, and then the two girls slung the wet water skins on their shoulders. It was a heavy load for both of them; Talia wondered how she could hurry back to her father. She nearly staggered under the weight. The sacks bumped against her rump and legs as she walked. Havilah helped her readjust them so they didn't slap so hard.

But it wasn't good enough. Talia simply could not keep up with her stronger cousin. Tears welled in her eyes as the straps of the heavy water skins cut into her shoulders. Finally Havilah told her she would go on ahead to find Uncle Yoktan and ask him to come back to help.

When Havilah was out of sight, Talia bent over to let the wet straps slide down her arms to the cobblestones. She stood to wipe her eyes and look about her.

She glimpsed a woman with silvered hair coming round a corner. She caught her breath. It was slender Aunt Selina.

"Aunt Selina!"

"Talia! What are you doing?"

"We—Papa and Havilah and I—have come for water and grain for our family. We are staying at Aunt Rahab's."

"Ah. Yes. Rahab." Aunt Selina seemed to spit the words out of her mouth.

"Hurry, Aunt Selina. Won't you come? Where is Yakesh?"

"We are not coming."

"But the army, Aunt Selina. It is circling again!"

"We are not coming," Aunt Selina repeated angrily.

Stunned, Talia stepped closer to talk with her aunt. "But you must come! The trumpets are blowing. Their army will conquer Jericho. Aunt Rahab has promised us a rescue."

"I do not believe my sister Rahab. The walls of Jericho will never be breached. Our gods will protect us."

In the distance, Talia heard the trumpets of the soldiers once again. Her heart seemed to thunder in her ears. She heard her father calling urgently: "Talia! Where are you? Come!"

Talia looked at her aunt. She began to cry. "Please, Aunt Selina. Won't you and Yakesh and Uncle Kedar come? I know in my heart that what Aunt Rahab says is true. Please, Aunt Selina."

"No, Talia, dear. I do not believe Rahab. She has been wrong too many times before. I will not come with you." Her sharp words dropped like shards of pottery to the cobblestones. She turned and walked away with quick little steps.

Talia's shoulders began to shake. As tears flowed freely down her brown cheeks, her father came beside her and held her close momentarily and then urged her forward.

Like the sound of the wild geese at harvest time crying the warning for winter, the trumpets blew again.

chapter eight

The Fall of Jericho

Talia, Havilah, and Papa ascended the dark stairs and arrived in the little tower room, perplexed and panting with their heavy loads. They were greeted with concerned relief—but such confusion. Everyone was talking at once!

Talia slid a water sack off her shoulder and wrapped her arms around her mother's waist. Papa and Mama exchanged the news that the army had now circled Jericho five times.

Within minutes of Talia's return to the tower, the horns heralded a sixth time. Everyone in the tower hushed. The tension was thick. It was midafternoon. It would not be long until dusk set in. Talia shivered, pulled her brown shawl up around her shoulders, and leaned harder into her mother's warmth.

Then she craned her neck to count the people—Mama, Papa holding Baka, Uncle Omar, Aunt Rahab and Havilah, another aunt and uncle, five more cousins, Saba and Sabta. She counted again. There were fifteen people, sixteen counting herself. Sixteen of her family with their sleeping mats and supplies all crowded into the same small space they had occupied for six long days. There wasn't room for anyone else.

Then she thought of her missing family members. There *was* room for more. Talia fought back hot tears.

Baka started to fuss. Papa shushed and rocked him the best he could, squeezed between Mama and big Uncle Omar.

The room was so warm, the air so still. But Talia couldn't help shaking. She was frightened. She and Havilah looked at each other. They asked each other questions without saying anything. What was going to happen?

The voices of people out on the top of the wall drifted through the window. They had resumed laughing and shouting at the army, mocking the discordant drone of the trumpets. Talia turned toward the noise. There was the bright red cord hanging over the windowsill. She sighed and closed her eyes.

Then she remembered the little bird's nest perched on the ledge on her way to the well, with the mama sparrow's wing spread over the baby birds to protect them from the wind. Talia pictured a big soft wing shielding her family in this tower room. She sighed again and opened her eyes.

It seemed hours that they all sat waiting, waiting. The cadence of the army's marching feet had faded once more, and the clamor from the people on the strong walls of Jericho had died down to quiet joking and chatter. Talia was hot and tired. She felt drowsy. It would feel good to stretch out on her sleeping mat and take a nap. Her thoughts drifted off to the flax field with its beautiful azure blooms.

But what was happening to their flax field? Were the soldiers trampling it down? Oh, no. The flowers.

Their field. Their linen business! Talia reached out to tug on Papa's shirt.

But just then the trumpets blew again. That eerie tone: "*Ta-ruah. Ta-ruah.*" She had heard it for seven days now, and this was the seventh time today. Why did they keep blowing those rams' horns? It was a terrible noise.

And then from below the walls came another sound, an awful outcry, a blood-curdling bellow. It was the battle cry of the army, louder than the rams' horns, more horrible than anything Talia had heard in her life. It seemed like the roar of a great lion ready to lunge at its prey.

The din echoed off the tower walls. It filled the air: yowls, bellows, pitched shouts and shrieks, a racket, a roar, and then silence. Talia and her family were all standing, rigid and alert.

It was quiet again. Talia could hear Havilah breathing in short choppy breaths next to her. Aunt Rahab shuffled her feet. Uncle Laban looked around the room. Mama's eyes locked on Talia's to reassure her and to tell her to stay quiet.

Then Talia heard another sound, a sound like thunder booming in mid-summer, like horses' hooves pounding across the plain, or like a thousand cattle and sheep stampeding into the walls of Jericho.

The uproar came to her in billowing clouds of noise that beat against her, slamming her ears, hitting her chest. She could barely breathe. She felt that it was pounding on her, that it would knock her over. The whole room began to shake. The rumble was right underneath their feet. Everyone held his breath. The floor shook; the walls shook; Talia shook. A pottery pitcher fell off a shelf behind her and smashed on the floor. A shard struck the back of her leg, and she felt a cool trickle of blood. She and Havilah found each other's hands and held on for dear life. They crowded in even closer to their cousins and aunts in front of them.

The room shook harder as the noise of smashing rocks reached them. It sounded like thunder and waterfalls and stampeding horses all mixed together. Smoke billowed into the room. Talia's legs were shaking; everything was shaking. Havilah squeezed her hand harder. Talia began to cry.

From outside the window, they heard people screaming and wailing. There were terrible sounds, sounds Talia had never even imagined. She let go of Havilah and put her hands over her ears, squeezing her eyes shut to help keep out the shrieks. Aunt Selina. Yakesh. What was happening to them? Was Jericho really falling to the invaders? What would happen to her, to all her family in this little tower room?

The uproar went on and on. Everyone in the room began to cough and choke on the smoke and dust coming in Aunt Rahab's window. Baka cried, but Papa didn't try to shush him anymore. No one could possibly hear him with all the rumble and racket going on out there.

Finally the sound and dust settled enough for Uncle Omar to look out the window. He seemed to gaze in horror for a long time. Then he turned with big eyes to his family and announced heavily, "The great walls of Jericho have fallen."

No one could believe it. Everyone started talking at once.

"No. It can't be!"

"How did they do it? What did they use?"

"Let me see. Let me see."

The rumbling had faded. It would almost stop, and then there would be the sound of another big boulder sliding and settling. They could hear weeping and shrieking for help. These sounds were sadder than the giant roar just a few moments before.

Talia opened her eyes and brought her hands to her sides. Havilah was crying hard. Talia coughed into her sleeve. A little cloud of gray puffed up when she moved her arm. She looked around at everyone. Drops of sweat were sliding down their faces, making shiny lines where the dust was washed away. Her aunts were weeping. She groped for Havilah's hand and found it again. Her palm was clammy, but comforting.

The walls of Jericho had fallen. The walls of Jericho had fallen? But they were so big and strong, so high and secure. How could this be? Who was this army?

And who was this God?

Still they waited. In spite of the warmth, Talia felt cold. She quivered as she waited in the awful silence.

A breeze blew in the window. It swept the dust from their hair, their shoulders, their chests. The dust swirled around the room, above their heads, and out the window, past the bright red cord.

The air was lighter. Talia felt freshened.

Then suddenly they heard shouting! It was the voice of triumph.

Talia looked around. Everyone's faces had frozen in fear once again. The alien army had triumphed. It was moving toward the once-mighty walls of Jericho.

And Talia and her family were trapped, alone, in this tiny tower room.

chapter nine

Under His Wings

The fuzzy dark head of a man suddenly appeared in the window. He seemed to be suspended in air. His face was framed above the scarlet cord, his eyes sparkling at them above a bushy beard. Was there no end to surprises this day?

"Come," he boomed. "Who will be first?"

Uncle Omar's and Papa's mouths dropped open as they gazed at this rescuer and then back at their family surrounding them in the crowded room. Everyone started talking at once, picking up energy and joy as they realized their release had come.

Aunt Rahab rushed to the window and greeted this man. She talked with him, nodding frequently, and then turned to explain to her family, "This man is an Israelite, one of the spies I hid several weeks ago. He and the other spy have come to take us down to safety. They have cut the limbs from a sycamore tree and leaned it below the window here. They will assist us in climbing down the tree ladder. Let us honor our father by allowing him to be the first to find freedom."

The men beckoned Saba to come to them, and they hoisted him up. The friendly man in the window reached down to lift Talia's old grandfather to the windowsill. Saba sat there a moment and then gathered his thin legs under him, turned to smile at his family, and began to disappear.

Aunt Rahab went next, followed by Sabta.

Talia was excited and dismayed at the same time. She had never looked out the high window, but she knew the ground must be a long way below. When it was her turn to be lifted to the sill, Papa held her tightly, kissed her on the cheek, and whispered, "All will be well, Talia. Do not be afraid. Don't look down. Take one step at a time. Our God who kept our tower standing will not forsake you now." His whispered words gave her the courage she needed.

Papa grasped Talia below her waist and swung her up to the man in the window. He smiled and said quietly, "Come, little one, we have a song about our God. 'Jehovah only is my rock and my salvation, my stronghold.' You can trust Him."

"Jehovah."

Jehovah. Was this the name of the God who had called her? It soothed her like the music of the breeze in her beloved flax field.

The flax field. Could she see it from this height? Talia glanced out the window, and the sight made her dizzy. She saw the boulders that had been the strong walls of Jericho piled in crazy mounds. The invading soldiers swarmed over them in pursuit of people and animals, slashing at them with their shining swords. It was horrible. Men shouted. People screamed. Blood stained many of the rocks. Below her, Talia saw a hand sticking out from under a boulder. She gagged and grabbed her stomach.

She looked away from the sight of war and beyond the plain below where tiny people gazed up at the tower. She saw the trees and mountains.

Talia shook her head. Papa had said, "Don't look down." She realized she was clutching the branch too tightly when the man laughed and said, "Let go, little monkey. Let me guide you. Take a step here." He moved below her on the tree ladder, never losing his grip around her brown tunic.

Slowly they descended until they reached a place halfway down where the ladder rested against fallen boulders that had formed a sort of stairway with giant steps when the wall collapsed. Other men were there, waiting to assist Talia and her family from boulder to boulder while the first man went back up the tree to the window. She looked up and saw Havilah waving at her. She would be the next to come down! And hanging from the window was the long scarlet cord, tangled and draped in the tree ladder like a festival decoration. Talia understood now. The red thread was the signal for their deliverance.

Below her Talia could see Saba and her aunt and others waiting for her descent. After days spent pent up in Aunt Rahab's tower, she felt like a little lizard, scurrying down from rock to rock with the help of these kind men. All the while, the new name was ringing in her ears, "Jehovah, Jehovah." It was a sound of joy. She would find a song to sing.

The men assisting Talia tried to shield her from the clamor and commotion, but she had to jump over a flow of blood in one place. She hesitated and then grabbed the helping hand hard and looked away, remembering her father's words, *All will be well, Talia. Do not be afraid. Our God who kept our tower standing will not forsake you now.*

At the bottom, Talia joined the remnant of her family who greeted her with open arms. They huddled together, but Talia shuddered. She had left her brown shawl behind and felt chilled after the excitement of leaving the tower.

Saba was resting on a rock with Sabta. He beckoned Talia to sit beside him. He put his arm around her and pulled her to his soft side. She leaned against him and cried as hard as she could. She shook and shivered and sobbed.

Finally she wiped her eyes and looked up at her grandpa. His eyes sparkled in his old wrinkled face as he gently lifted her chin and said, "Talia, you will remember this day all your life. The mighty God of a great people has rescued us. We should be deeply grateful."

"Oh, Saba, I am! And did you hear his name? Jehovah."

"Yes, Talia. I heard."

Talia nestled beside him as they watched the rest of their family descend. She was exhausted from the long day's events. She had nearly dozed off when Havilah tapped her on her arm.

Talia blinked her eyes. Saba was smiling down at her. Havilah was urging her to get up. Night was coming.

"Talia—look. We are all here. Look. People are coming toward us. Let's go meet them."

A group of women and children were approaching. The children were laughing and skipping. Many of their mothers were carrying lanterns, their lamp-lit shawls looking like wispy clouds on a starry night. And they were singing.

"Be strong! Be courageous!
Jehovah is at our side.

Be strong! Be courageous!
Jehovah Jireh will provide.
Do not fear. Be not dismayed.
The Lord thy God is here.
Do not fear. Be not afraid.
Jehovah is our God. Hey!"

Talia hummed the new song as the two groups drew closer together. Some children carried tambourines that sounded so bright in the gathering darkness. The party encircled Talia's family with their lights and lyrics. When the song ended, the singers embraced them with hugs and cheers and blessings.

"Welcome, welcome, dear ones."

"In the name of our great Jehovah, we greet you."

"Come, you must be tired. We will give you food."

A girl Talia's size with long dark curls shyly came up to her. "My name is Sarah."

"My name is Talia."

They smiled at each other. Sarah slipped her arm through Talia's and walked beside her. They looked at each other and laughed.

"Were you afraid?" Sarah asked.

"Oh, yes!" Talia answered. "It has been a long, hard time. I have been frightened. We left everything behind. I do not even have my shawl. And—my cousin. My aunt and uncle . . ." Talia choked back her tears.

"I am so sorry, Talia. But now you are free. Jehovah will watch over you. He has watched over us. He has done miracles!"

"Yes—I—I believe you. He protected my whole family. And I am glad to know His name, His beautiful name—*Jehovah*."

Havilah joined the girls and clasped Talia's free hand. The three walked in the twilight toward a fire Sarah's people had prepared for them. Others were there, cooking a meal. It smelled rich and roasty. When those around the fire saw the group approach, they also got up to greet Rahab's family.

Talia found her way through the joyous clamor to Mama, Papa, and Baka. He stretched his short arms out to his sister, saying, "Taly, Taly, Baka go down big twee!"

Talia laughed as she squeezed his hands and then hugged her parents and cried, "Papa, we are free!"

Papa leaned down to look his daughter in the eyes. "Yes, Talia, and I am so proud of you. You have been brave and have believed in our new God."

"Yes, Papa. Did you hear His name? Did you hear them singing? His name is Jehovah. Jehovah Jireh."

"Yes, Talia. I heard."

Talia threw her arms around Papa's strong neck and cried on his shoulder. Gently he pushed her away and urged her, "Come. They have prepared food for us. Let us eat, and then perhaps we can all rest."

A big tent had been set up for Rahab's whole family. After the good meal, they chose their places on sleeping pallets. Havilah, Talia, and Baka cuddled up together.

Talia had nearly dozed off when she heard a whisper just above her head.

"Talia."

Her new friend Sarah had tiptoed into the tent. "I was afraid you would be cold. I brought my shawl for you. Let me spread it out." As the garment floated above her and came down to warm Havilah and Baka as well as herself, Sarah whispered, "May the Lord, the God of Israel, under Whose wings you have come to seek refuge, bless you, and guard you in the night."

"Thank you, Sarah. Thank you! Good night."

"Good night, Talia."

Talia heard Sarah sneak out of the tent and scurry away in the sand to her own place inside the Israelite camp. Talia felt blanketed in love and security. She fell into a deep and restful sleep.

In the morning, as the sun rose, she stirred and saw Baka sleeping peacefully beside her. All of a sudden she remembered where she was and what had happened. She sat up to look around.

There were Mama and Papa nearby. There were Aunt Rahab and the rest of her dear family. And here she was beside Baka and Havilah. They had been covered in a warm wool shawl by a new friend.

And now she could see that the shawl was blue, the blue of her beloved flax.

Jehovah-Jireh. The Lord provides.

"Thank you," Talia whispered. "Thank you, Jehovah."

She sighed deeply and returned to rest under her new blue shawl.

Pronunciation Guide

Talia	TAH-lyah
Aunt Rahab	RAH-hahv
Yoktan	YOKE-tahn
Hanah	HAH-nah
Baka	BAH-kah
Saba	SAH-bah
Sabta	SAHB-tah
Heth	HETH
Havilah	Hah-VEE-lah
Uncle Omar	OH-mahr
Aunt Selina	seh-LEE-nah
Uncle Kedar	kay-DAHR
Cousin Yakesh	YAH-kaysh
Kaleb	kah-LAYB
Sarah	SAH-rah

From the Author

The amazing story of the fall of Jericho is found in the Bible in chapters 2–6 of Joshua. I encourage you to read it.

Talia, Havilah, and Baka are not mentioned there, but Rahab and her family are. I love the story so much that I imagined what relatives she might have had and what their lives might have been like in ancient Jericho—over thirty-four hundred years ago!

Joshua 2:6 says that Rahab hid the spies on her rooftop under stalks of flax, the plant that is used to make linen cloth. That detail made me think that some of Rahab's relatives might have been a flax farmer and linen weaver, so I created Talia and her family.

I decided to learn about the ancient technology of growing and processing flax, and of dyeing and weaving linen. I researched books and interviewed some knowledgeable people. I saw a flax demonstration at the Farmer's Museum in Cooperstown, New York, and I even grew flax in our garden.

I had to imagine what it would have been like to live inside a walled city where people believed in false gods instead of in the one true God. The Bible tells us He is a God of love and holiness Who cares about every single person. Isaiah 43:1 says that God has created us and called us by name. He knows *your* name.

In the story Talia heard God calling her. Do you hear God calling you? He wants you to know Him. A long time after the story of Jericho, God sent His Son, Jesus, to earth to teach us about Himself and to do miracles. Jesus died on a cross for our sins so that God would not have to punish us. The greatest miracle of all is that He rose from the dead. His death removed the wall of sin that separates us from God.

Talia came to believe that there was a real God to trust, and she came under His wings of protection. God wants you to come to Him through Jesus. Acts 16:31 promises that if you believe in the Lord Jesus, you will be saved. I hope you will believe in Him and come under His wings.

If you have questions about God's promise or about Talia's adventures, I hope you will write to me at blueshawl@stny.rr.com. I would love to hear from you.

Love,
Ginny Merritt

Acknowledgements

Teamwork goes into the writing of a book, and I have many team members to thank.

First of all, I want to acknowledge what a rich source of inspiration, instruction, and friendships the Montrose Christian Writers Conference in Montrose, Pennsylvania, has been to me for many years. I thank the Fahringers, the Kosiks, the Wymbs, the Odd Ducks, and the Not-So-Odd Ducks for making the conference possible. Most especially, I thank the directors, Patti Souder and Carol Wedeven, godly guides, funny friends, and source of "yeller pencils with erasers."

This book has required a good bit of research, and I thank Dr. David Dorsey from Evangelical School of Theology in Myerstown, Pennsylvania, and Ariel and D'vorah Berkowitz of Torah Resources International, friends of old. All three have helped me over and again with "just one more question."

My practitioner, Diana Shaw, helped me think through a sticky medical problem. Laughter is good medicine.

Most of the wonderful Emhoff family sat and listened to a first reading of *The Window in the Wall.* Thank you, Donalu, Elisabeth, Josiah, Will, and Louisa (my "model" for Talia). Jeff, Adoniram, and Sasha were working, playing, or sleeping.

My husband, Ray, made dinner or cleared the table when I had a deadline. Our daughter, Ann Elyse, was a ruthless editor (thanks, AE). Our son, Hans, and his sons Odin and Cyrus cheered me on in my writing. Cyrus wouldn't go to sleep until I read the final chapter to him.

My editor, Nancy Lohr, is the best. She's also the "only," but we've discussed that. She is thorough, encouraging, instructive, kind, and fun. What more could anyone want in an editor?

I have a group of prayer partners I call my "Book Boosters." Thank you, Lisa Berryment (sweeeeeet), Marilyn Blodgett (dear sister), AE (Merci, Mme. Foltz), Joyce Hickling (prayers going ^), Shirl Leonard (you're my friend), Kristine Reid (wahoo!), Patti Souder (you are SO amazing!), Carol Wedeven (anybody see a Conestoga wagon?), Linda Willmott (have you seen the movie yet?), and Pat Woolever (FOCUS).

And I am grateful for an extra encourager, Christine Lindberg, warrior of words and woodchucks.

My parents gave me a love for life and learning. My mom, Sally, whistled even while she washed dishes and greeted us with eyes that sparkled. My dad, Owen Billman, had a head full of marvelous ideas and amazing unfinished projects, but he always had time to play with me and my siblings, Carol, Jan, and Steve. Mom and Dad would have loved Talia's story.

I thank a host of other friends and family who have prayed for me, encouraged me, and kept me in line.

I thank Sue and Merle Ayers and the staff of the Clyde-Savannah Public Library for letting me use the back room and keeping me online.

Most of all, I thank my God—Father, Son, and Holy Spirit— for my life, my salvation, my hope of heaven. I thank Him that at Talia's age I heard His voice. May this book and all I do be for His glory and the building of His kingdom.

Thank you. Thank you, Jehovah.